The
Vanguard

ARNOLD BENNETT

By ARNOLD BENNETT

NOVELS

THE VANGUARD
THE WOMAN WHO STOLE EVERY-
    THING
LORD RAINGO
ELSIE AND THE CHILD
RICEYMAN STEPS
LILIAN
MR. PROHACK
THE ROLL-CALL
THE PRETTY LADY
THE LION'S SHARE
THESE TWAIN
CLAYHANGER
HILDA LESSWAYS
THE OLD WIVES' TALE
DENRY THE AUDACIOUS

THE OLD ADAM
HELEN WITH THE HIGH HAND
THE GATES OF WRATH
THE BOOK OF CARLOTTA
BURIED ALIVE
A GREAT MAN
LEONORA
WHOM GOD HATH JOINED
A MAN FROM THE NORTH
ANNA OF THE FIVE TOWNS
THE GLIMPSE
THE GRAND BABYLON HOTEL
HUGO
THE CITY OF PLEASURE
THE MATADOR OF THE FIVE
    TOWNS

POCKET PHILOSOPHIES

HOW TO MAKE THE BEST OF
    LIFE
SELF AND SELF MANAGEMENT
MARRIED LIFE
FRIENDSHIP AND HAPPINESS
THE HUMAN MACHINE

HOW TO LIVE ON 24 HOURS A
    DAY
LITERARY TASTE
MENTAL EFFICIENCY
THE AUTHOR'S CRAFT

PLAYS

THE LOVE MATCH
BODY AND SOUL
SACRED AND PROFANE LOVE
JUDITH
THE TITLE
THE BRIGHT ISLAND

THE GREAT ADVENTURE
CUPID AND COMMONSENSE
WHAT THE PUBLIC WANTS
POLITE FARCES
THE HONEYMOON
DON JUAN DE MARANA

IN COLLABORATION WITH EDWARD KNOBLOCK

MILESTONES

LONDON LIFE

MISCELLANEOUS

OUR WOMEN
BOOKS AND PERSONS
PARIS NIGHTS

LIBERTY
THE TRUTH ABOUT AN AUTHOR
OVER THERE: WAR SCENES

THINGS THAT HAVE INTERESTED ME
THINGS THAT HAVE INTERESTED ME. *Second Series*
THINGS THAT HAVE INTERESTED ME. *Third Series*

NEW YORK: GEORGE H. DORAN COMPANY

THE VANGUARD

A Fantasia by

ARNOLD BENNETT

THE LITERARY GUILD
OF AMERICA

NEW YORK   MCMXXVII

CONTENTS

The Vanguard

The Vanguard

CHAPTER I

THE SPLENDIDE

Mr. Sutherland rang the bell once, in his private sitting-room at the Hotel Splendide, and expected the prompt arrival of the waiter. Mr. Sutherland was a man of fifty, clean-shaven, spare, rather austere, with the responsible and slightly harassed demeanour which comes of having married young and remained married, and the thin lips and logical jaw which usually develop on the faces of men who have been called to the bar. Brown-grey hair that might soon, but not yet, be described as scanty. Pale blue eyes, whose glance denoted a certain mild self-complacency on the part of Mr. Sutherland. The reasons for the self-complacency were various and sound.

In the first place, Mr. Sutherland was a seventh child: to be which is always a mystical asset in life, and further, his parents had indicated his ordinal position in their family by christening him, not Septimus, which is banal, but Septimius, which is rare and distinguished. That extra "i" had virtue for Mr. Sutherland.

In the second place, Mr. Sutherland some thirty years earlier had stroked the Cambridge boat. Nobody, in giving an account of Mr. Sutherland to people who were unacquainted with him, ever omitted to mention this fact, and only cynical or malign persons would mention also that he had not stroked Cambridge to victory.

The third reason for self-complacency was that Mr. Sutherland was, and knew himself to be, an organizer. He organized everything in his existence and when, as now, he was enjoying for a space the absence of his delicious, disorganizing wife and girls, and of a devoted, incompetent valet, he would organize with abandonment and utterly revel in his talent for organizing.

The apartment gave evidences of organization. Mr. Sutherland was leaving the city that evening by train. The receipted bill, much stamped, for his sojourn at the Splendide lay open on the centre table. His suitcase lay open on a side-table, with a couple of books all ready to slip into it. The suitcase was labelled with two labels, one adhesive, the other attached by string. In the bedroom lay Mr. Sutherland's flat American trunk, still open, lest Mr. Sutherland might have forgotten something. It could be snapped to in a second. Hanging over the raised lid of the trunk (which had three labels) was Mr. Sutherland's rug, conveniently folded, and on an adjacent chair were his hat, overcoat, and gloves. The spectacle of all this organized order gave pleasure to Mr. Sutherland.

The bell was not answered. Mr. Sutherland's organization, however, was not disconcerted by the delay. He always allowed a margin for the imperfections of mankind and the malice of heaven; and now he utilized this margin by systematically opening every drawer in the sitting-room, bedroom, and bathroom, and demonstrating to himself, for the second time, that he had forgotten nothing. Thereupon he shut the American trunk.

Still the bell was not answered. And now Mr. Sutherland began to have a new and dark idea about the organization of the Hotel Splendide, which organization he had hitherto admired without reserve. The Splendide was the best hotel in the city. There were four other leading and in every way first-class hotels—the Majestic, the Belvidere, the Royal Palace, and the Grand Miramar, and according to advertisement each of these four was also the best hotel in the city. The Splendide, however, had two advantages over its rivals—due to two discoveries made by its designers. The first discovery was that the visitor does not care to overhear everything that passes, by word or action, in the rooms adjoining his own, or even in the corridor; and the second was that the visitor finds little pleasure in the continual sounding of a bell—once for the waiter, twice for the chambermaid, and thrice for the valet—especially when the rung bell is situate, as it always is, just outside his bedroom door. Hence the designers of the Splendide had established double doors between adjoining rooms and between rooms and corridor, and had entirely done away with the sound of bells. When you pushed the button at the Splendide—the top one for the waiter, the middle one for the chambermaid, and the lower one for the valet—a white, a green, or a red light shone in the corridor above your door and kept on shining until the waiter, the chambermaid, or the valet (duly warned by a bell far, far out of hearing of the visitor) came and extinguished it. Thus, if you closed your double windows, you could live at the Splendide as in the isolated silence and select privacy of the grave, until you died from steam-heat and lack of ventilation.

It was all most ingenious, and Mr. Sutherland had loved it all. But now he perceived a psychological flaw in this organization. The visitor, having rung without getting a reply, could not be sure whether or not the apparatus was in order. Supposing the distant bell was for some reason not functioning! A terrible thought! Mr. Sutherland, after a further pause, opened the double doors into the corridor and looked forth. Yes, the white light, symbolic of his desire for the waiter, was burning over his door and burning brightly, steadily, patiently, waiting for the waiter. But had the bell rung? Mr. Sutherland could not and did not know. He did not even know where the bell was to be found. Silence and solitude in the long corridor! Dozens of doors, and only one of them illuminated, Mr. Sutherland's!

Septimius felt himself to be a victim, and yet somehow guilty; the white light seemed to accuse him of something. He was at a loss. He knew not what to do. His great gift for organizing had been rendered futile. He hesitated, most absurdly, to step out into the hostile wilderness of the corridor. At last he did step out, and it was as though he had gone over the top in battle. Then Mr. Sutherland saw a waiter in the distance, and stepped back into the ambush of the doorway and halted the waiter at the moment of passing the door. The waiter, startled out of his professional self-control, gave Septimius a look of murderous hatred. The glance covered perhaps the tenth of a second, and was instantaneously succeeded by the conventional acquiescent smile of his calling;

but Septimius had noted it, and was afraid in his heart, for the glance seemed to symbolize and lay bare the awful secret antagonism which divides the servers from the served—seed of revolutions. Septimius even feared for his life, for he was in a strange and sinister city, where lives were worth much less than in London, and some people might possibly find their advantage in the sudden death of Septimius . . . Pooh! Ridiculous!

"Please bring me the menu," Mr. Sutherland, speaking in English, addressed the waiter, whom he had never seen before. And he carefully spoke as one man to another, in order to indicate his belief in the dogma that all men are equal before heaven. "I shall dine here in my room. And when you serve the dinner let me have the bill with it—receipted. You understand. I'm leaving to-night."

The waiter smiled charmingly to indicate his belief in the dogma that the least wish of a visitor is a law to the waiter. He smiled, bowed, and departed. He had understood only two words, "menu" and "bill."

Mr. Sutherland felt reassured, though he had had a shock.

After a brief delay the waiter returned, without the menu, and made quite a long foreign speech to Mr. Sutherland, not a word of which did Mr. Sutherland comprehend. The black-coated fellow was one of those waiters, prevalent in the splendid hotels of distant and picturesque lands, who can speak no language but their own, and sometimes not even that. Ten key-words of English or French may suffice a waiter for the common affair of human nature's daily food, but in a crisis they quickly prove inadequate.

Mr. Sutherland saw that this was a crisis. He could

speak Sutherland-French, slowly, and he now did so. But the waiter's face was an amiable blank before the persuasions of Sutherland-French.

"Menu, menu, menu! Carte, carte, carte!" Mr. Sutherland repeated firmly and kindly, but foolishly.

The waiter shook his head. At last Mr. Sutherland in blank despair waved him from the room.

"Is it conceivable," thought Septimius, "that in a hotel with the pretentions of the Splendide, they should place you at the mercy of servants with whom it is impossible to communicate?" He saw that it was conceivable, and sighed.

There was only one thing to do—namely to adventure forth into the general publicity and promiscuity of the vast hotel. The necessity for so doing oppressed Mr. Sutherland strangely.

CHAPTER II

THE STRIKE

THE two principal public rooms of the Splendide were the lounge and the restaurant. They lay side by side, separated by a wall of glass, and they were both vast and both ultra- or super-gorgeous. Every square foot of their walls and ceilings was decorated with the last extreme of ornateness in either oils, fresco, mosaic, porphyry, gilt, or bronze. On the ceiling alone, of the lounge, were depicted, in various mediums, over seventy slim and beautiful young women in a high state of physical development and chiefly in the fashion of Eden, perilously tasting the dubious society of thirty or forty fauns and satyrs whose moral code seemed to illustrate the joyous effrontery of a past age and who had no preoccupations about rates, taxes, bad weather, or class-warfare. The colours of this ideal world were rich, fresh, and brilliant, for it was only in the previous year that the designers had finished spending two million lire in the creation of the Splendide: which was meant to respond, and indeed did respond, to the secret aspirations of the élite of Cincinnati, Leeds, Buenos Ayres, Philadelphia, Bath and Boston (Mass).

From the lounge, through the gilded crystal partition, could be seen the equally opulent restaurant, full of tables richly set with napery, cutlery, glass, and flowers, and perambulated by many restless waiters. And not one diner at any of the tables, though the hour was after half-past eight!

While the forlorn restaurant held waiters but no guests, the lounge held guests but no waiters. Twenty-three guests were congregated together in the middle of the huge parqueted floor upon which, on normal evenings, they were accustomed to dance. A small number for so large an hotel; but the season had scarcely started; moreover, the Splendide much depended for its customers upon the arrival and departure of Transatlantic and Transmediterranean steamers, and no important boat had arrived or departed now for several days. The present guests were chiefly not mere migrants but steady supporters of the hotel and the city, whose purpose was to stay, and see, and leave quantities of good money behind them. Of the twenty-three, fifteen were American, five English, and the rest of doubtful origin; seventeen were women and the rest men. Their anxious and perturbed demeanour was in dismal contrast with that of the gaudy, carefree inhabitants of the ceiling-kingdom overhead.

Alone among them a tall, dark, massive, romantic gentleman of forty years or so seemed to be enjoying life. He was fat, and it might have been said that the pores of his stretched skin, being open, exuded gaiety, and that gaiety escaped frothing from his lips. As, lightly, with little mincing steps of his small toes, he moved about gesticulating and chatting with an inner group of ladies, he had the air of being continuously animated by a private and particular zest of his own. His manner was easy and affable to the point of patronage, for he knew that he was adored.